T 7

D0458830

WITHDR

DATE DUE

JUN 2 0 1998	JUL 1 1 2011	
JUN 2 7 1998	FEB 2 8 2017	
OCT 2 8 2000	NOV 1 5 2017	
FEB 0 9 2005	JUN 2 7 2018	
NOV 2 1 2005		
JUN. 2 2 2007		
JAN 1 2 2008		
JAN 3 1 2008		
NOV 1 9 2009		
JUL 0 8 2011		

E
Mar

Mariconda, Barbara
Witch way to the beach

Grant Public Library
Grant, NE 69140

MEDIALOG INC
ALEXANDRIA KY 41001

WITCH WAY TO THE BEACH

WITCH WAY TO THE BEACH

Barbara Mariconda

illustrated by Jon McIntosh

A Yearling First Choice Chapter Book

To Mariann Hudak, painter of dreams,
with love and gratitude   —B.M.

For Jeannie
—J.M.

Published by
Bantam Doubleday Dell Publishing Group, Inc.
1540 Broadway
New York, New York 10036

Text copyright © 1997 by Barbara Mariconda
Illustrations copyright © 1997 by Jon McIntosh
All rights reserved.

If you purchased a paperback edition of this book without a cover you should be aware that this book is stolen property. It was reported as "unsold and destroyed" to the publisher and neither the author nor the publisher has received any payment for this "stripped book."

Library of Congress Cataloging-in-Publication Data
Mariconda, Barbara.
    Witch way to the beach / Barbara Mariconda ; illustrated by Jon McIntosh.
        p. cm.
    "A Yearling first choice chapter book."
    Summary: City witch Drusilla and country witch Constance ride a vacuum cleaner to the beach, where they hope to have fun despite Constance's dislike of beaches.
    ISBN 0-385-32265-8 (alk. paper). —ISBN 0-440-41268-4 (pbk. : alk. paper)
    [1. Witches—Fiction.   2. Beaches—Fiction.]   I. McIntosh, Jon, ill.
II. Title.
PZ7.M33835Wi   1997
[E]—dc20
                                            96-34400
                                            CIP
                                            AC

Hardcover: The trademark Delacorte Press® is registered in the
U.S. Patent and Trademark Office and in other countries.
Paperback: The trademark Yearling® is registered in the
U.S. Patent and Trademark Office and in other countries.

The text of this book is set in 17-point Baskerville.
Book design by Trish Parcell Watts
Manufactured in the United States of America
June 1997
10   9   8   7   6   5   4   3   2   1

17485

CONTENTS

1.
A GREAT DAY
FOR A BROOM RIDE

Constance sat by the window.

Her myna bird, Myrna,

sat by the window too.

"It's a great day for a broom ride,"

said Constance.

Whoosh, came a sound from the sky.

"That sounds like my cousin Drusilla,"
said Constance.

"It sounds like her vacuum cleaner."

"It sounds like trouble," said Myrna.

Drusilla and her cat, Hiss,

flew in the window.

That was the good news.

7

The bad news was that
the window was not open.
Crash! went the window.
They landed on the broom!
Crack! went the broom handle.
Snap! went the broom bristles.
"It's not a great day for a broom
ride anymore," said Constance.
"Hello, Cousin!" sang Drusilla.
"I have come from the city to
take you on a trip."
"Hello, Drusilla," said Constance.
"I do not want to go on a trip.
I wanted to go on a broom ride."

Hiss looked at the broken handle.

Drusilla looked at the broken bristles.

"You cannot go on a broom ride,"

said Drusilla.

"You do not have a broom!

And besides," added Drusilla,

"a trip is more fun than a broom ride."

Constance shook her head.

"A trip to where?" she asked.

"To the beach!" said Drusilla.

"It will be fun!"

"Hiss!" said Hiss.

"Trouble!" said Myrna.

"It will NOT be fun," said Constance.

"I do not like the sun.

I do not like the sand.

I do not like the water."

"But you will LOVE the beach!"

said Drusilla.

It was no use!

Drusilla would not give up.

"Don't worry," said Drusilla

as they got on the vacuum.

"What could possibly go wrong?"

Whoosh! went the vacuum.

They flew out the door.

That was the good news.

The bad news was that

the door was not open.

2.
SUN, SAND, AND WATER

Drusilla parked the vacuum.

Myrna and Hiss went off to play.

"I will find a place for us," said Drusilla.

She found a spot on the sand.

She waved to Constance.

Constance took chairs and umbrellas.

She took blankets and baskets.

She took shovels and buckets.

"This is one more reason I do not

like the beach," said Constance.

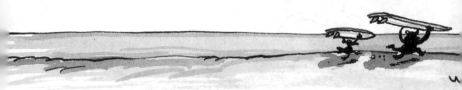

They sat in their chairs.

Constance yawned.

"We just got here," said Drusilla.

"I do not see why you are so tired."

Constance did not hear her.

She was asleep in the sun.

Constance does not like the sun,

thought Drusilla.

I know what to do.

Drusilla took sand.

Lots and lots of sand.

She covered Constance!

"There," said Drusilla.

"Now Constance will not feel the sun."

Constance woke up.

She could not feel the sun.

That was the good news.

The bad news was that

she could not feel her arms.

She could not feel her legs.

"Help! Help!" yelled Constance.

"I am sinking in the sand!"

The lifeguard jumped from his chair.
"I will save you!" he said.
He took the sand off Constance.
Constance still had sand
between her fingers.

She had sand between her toes.

She had sand between her teeth.

She had sand between her clothes.

Constance turned to Drusilla.

"Why did you cover me

with sand?" she asked.

"I covered you with sand

to keep out the sun," said Drusilla.

"The sun is nice compared

to this sand," said Constance.

Drusilla smiled.

"I KNEW you would like the sun!"

she said.

The sun DID feel good!

It made Constance sleepy.

She fell asleep. Again.

Constance does not like the sand,

thought Drusilla.

I know what to do.

Drusilla dug a ditch.

She dug it all the way to the water.

She dug it all the way

around Constance.

"There," said Drusilla.

"When the tide comes in,

Constance will not feel the sand!"

The tide came in.

Water filled the ditch.

It covered Constance.

It covered her book.

It covered her chair.

It covered her clothes.

It covered her hair.

The water washed the sand away.

That was the good news.

The bad news was that it

washed Constance away too!

"Help! Help!" yelled Constance.

"I am sinking in the water!"

"I will save you!" said the lifeguard.

He pulled Constance out of the water.

Constance turned to Drusilla.

"Why did you cover me with water?"

22

"I covered you with water
to wash away the sand,"
said Drusilla.
"The sand is nice compared
to this water!" said Constance.
Drusilla smiled.
"I KNEW you would like
the sand!" she said.
Constance dug her toes in the sand.

The sand DID feel good!

It made Constance sleepy.

For the third time, she fell asleep!

Constance does not like the water,

thought Drusilla.

I know what to do.

Drusilla got her vacuum.

Whoosh! went the vacuum.

It sucked up the water on Constance.

That was the good news.

The bad news was that

it sucked up other things too!

It sucked up the lifeguard's lunch!

It sucked up the lifeguard's towel!

It sucked up the lifeguard's

swimming trunks!

The lifeguard ran to the water.

"Help! Help!" yelled Constance.

"I am being sucked up
by this vacuum!"

"I cannot help you this time!"
said the lifeguard.

Drusilla turned off the vacuum.

Constance turned to Drusilla.

"Why did you use your

vacuum on me?" she asked.

"I used my vacuum to suck

up the water," said Drusilla.

"The water is nice compared

to this vacuum!" said Constance.

Drusilla smiled.

"I KNEW you would like the water!"
she said.

"And you were right!" said Constance.

"I like the sun!

I like the sand!

I like the water!"

"I guess that means
you like the beach!" said Drusilla.

"I am glad we came," said Constance.

"I am glad we came," said Drusilla.

"I am NOT glad you came!"
said the lifeguard.

3.
ALL WASHED UP

Hiss and Myrna came back.

They had had enough playing.

Drusilla sat back.

She had had enough tanning.

"Let's pack our things
and go," she said.

"Wait!" said Constance.

"I have just learned to like the sun!

I have just learned to like the sand!

I have just learned to like the water!

I want to stay and have fun!"

Drusilla sighed.

Myrna sighed.

Hiss hissed.

"Okay," said Drusilla.

"But make it fast!"

"Fast!" repeated Myrna.

Constance DID have fun!

She had fun in the sun.

She put on lotion.

She put on sunglasses.

She tanned her front.

She flipped over.

She tanned her back.

"Look at my suntan!" said Constance.

"Your suntan is very nice,"
said Drusilla.

"NOW can we go?"

"Not yet," said Constance.

"I want to have fun in the sand!"

"Okay," said Drusilla.

"But make it fast!"

"Fast!" repeated Myrna.

Constance DID have fun!

She picked up her pointy hat.

She filled her hat with sand.

She flipped it over.

She made pointy sand castles.

"Look at my sand castles!"

said Constance.

"Your castles are nice,"

said Drusilla.

"NOW can we go?"

Constance stopped.

"I want to have fun in
the water," she said.
"But we can have more fun
in the water together."
"Okay," said Drusilla,
"let's go have fun!"
They DID have fun.
They went on the float.

They splashed at the lifeguard.

They swam underwater.

They jumped over waves.

Then a big wave came.

A really, really big wave!

It took them on a wild ride.

A really, really wild ride!

It washed them up on the shore.

That was the good news.

The bad news was

that it washed up crabs.

It washed up jellyfish.

It washed up seaweed.

It washed up the lifeguard.

"I do NOT like these crabs!"

said Drusilla.

She pulled them off.

"I do NOT like these jellyfish!"

said Constance.

She pushed them away.

"I DO like this seaweed!"

said the lifeguard.

And he left it right where it was!

4.
FILL 'ER UP

Drusilla looked at Constance.
"Have you had your fill
of the beach?" she asked.
"I am tan," said Constance.
"I am sandy and I am wet."
"But I am also hungry!"
"Okay," said Drusilla.
"Let's go eat!"

They called the lifeguard.
"We will buy you an ice cream
for your trouble," said Constance.
They marched to the snack bar
and got in line.
"Ice cream cones for everyone!"
sang Drusilla.
The man gave Drusilla her cone.

Slurp, slurp.

Myrna got her cone. *Peck, peck.*

Hiss got his cone. *Lick, lick.*

The lifeguard got his cone. *Yum, yum.*

Constance stepped up for her cone.

"I am sorry," said the man,

"but we just ran out of cones!"

Constance looked at the others.

She looked at their pointy cones.

Constance had an idea!

She took off her pointy hat

and handed it to the man.

"Fill 'er up!" she said.

The man filled it up.

He filled and filled and filled it up!

Constance got her cone.

Gobble, gobble.

It was time to go.

They packed up their things.

Drusilla flew the vacuum around.

"Fill 'er up!" she said.

They piled on their things.

They piled and piled
and piled on their things.

Whoosh! went the vacuum.

They waved goodbye to the sun.

They waved goodbye to the sand.

They waved goodbye to the water.

They waved goodbye to the lifeguard.

That was the good news.

The bad news was that the lifeguard
waved goodbye to his ice cream!

"It was NOT a good day for a
broom ride," said Constance.

"And it was NOT a good day
for the lifeguard," said Drusilla.
"But," they said together,
"it was a GREAT day for the beach!"

BARBARA MARICONDA is also the author of *Witch Way to the Country*. She lives in Connecticut with her husband, two children, and one very large poodle.

JON MCINTOSH is also the illustrator of *Witch Way to the Country*. He has been an illustrator and designer for the past twenty-five years. He lives on the island of Martha's Vineyard.